KARATE FUN
at the Beach

ROBERT MCGRIFF &
KAILA MONET PACHECO
ILLUSTRATED BY: RICHA KINRA

Outskirts Press, Inc.
http://www.outskirtspress.com

ISBN: 978-1-9772-3725-5

Illustrated by: Richa Kinra
Illustrations © 2021 Outskirts Press, Inc. All rights reserved - used with permission.

Outskirts Press and the "OP" logo are trademarks belonging to Outskirts Press, Inc.

PRINTED IN THE UNITED STATES OF AMERICA

This Book Belongs to:

_____

Hi, my name is Kaila and I am six years old. My dad is the chief instructor at our karate school.

Today we are excited to be at the beach at sunrise to do karate walking with Junior Black Belt Mrs. Cook.

"What is karate walking?" asks Mrs. Cook.

"It is doing a count of five, ten, fifteen, or twenty karate skills in a row and walking forward between sets," she explains.

"The karate skills can be kicking, punching, or blocking," says Mrs. Cook.

"Sometimes my dad will do karate walking for up to a half of a mile," I tell her.

The group is thrilled about karate walking on the beach.

"The first thing we must do is stretch," says Mrs. Cook, "Let's begin our stretching."

"Now that we have stretched and warmed up properly, we can start karate walking. First we bow," Mrs. Cook instructs.

As I rise up from my bow, I see turtles-sea turtles! I yell with excitement. "Those are newly hatched sea turtles racing to the safety of the ocean," says Mrs. Cook in amazement.

"We are doing five back leg side kicks in a row. This is a power kick that can be used when you're attacked from the front," Mrs. Cook tells us.

"Next we do five front leg kicks. We use this kick for speed and aim for the stomach and lower body when a person is coming toward you," she explains.

As we complete the set of front leg kicks, we take time to look at the beautiful houses and their bright colors.

"Now it's time to do right leg side kicks. I will show you. This kick has enough power to break a board in half!" exclaims Mrs. Cook.

"Let's do the front leg side kick now. This is an awesome move. It is best used for an opponent who is moving toward you quickly," Mrs. Cook says.

"Look, we are so close to the pier now!"
says Amanda.

"Now we will begin the back leg roundhouse kicks. This skill is very good for kicking high," Mrs. Cook explains.

I feel the sand rushing from underneath my shoes as the water surges in and out. It is much cooler down here. The waves are roaring as they hit the pier post.

"Let's move on to the head block. This is great for protecting the top of your head from an overhead strike," Mrs. Cook says.

"The first part of the down block is to put your left arm over your right arm in the X position over your chest. This is used for protecting your chest and stomach," she says.

"The second part of down block is to bring the left arm down over the left knee. This skill will protect the lower body," explains Mrs. Cook.

We look out into the ocean and see a pod of dolphins swimming beside us. We stop to watch them as they swim past.

"Now we will do lunge punches. This move is used to practice balance and timing," Mrs. Cook says.

"Next we will practice a palm strike. This is used for self-defense when an attacker is close," Mrs. Cook tells us.

"Moving into the spear finger, this is also used when your attacker is close," she says.

There are seagulls flying overhead. There are
many seagulls
flying around
us this
morning.

Amanda and I take a moment to stop and enjoy the loudness of the ocean and the smell of the clean, salty air.

I look around and see all of the smiling faces. They are having fun and so are we.

All of us love karate walking, especially on the beach at sunrise.

We make it back to the beginning spot. This means our karate walking is complete, and we turn to Mrs. Cook and bow.

The End

Lightning Source UK Ltd.
Milton Keynes UK
UKHW050627100521
383284UK00003B/58